THE
BOY
IN THE BIG
BLACK
BOX

Written by Rebecca Lisle
Illustrated by Tim Archbold

For Frederika Klimas – RL
To Rosie and John – TA

First published in Great Britain in 2007
by Andersen Press Limited
20 Vauxhall Bridge Road
London SW1V 2SA
www.andersenpress.co.uk
www.rebeccalisle.com

British Library Cataloguing in Publication Data available.

ISBN 978 184 270 681 7

Printed in the UK by CPI Bookmarque, Croydon, CR0 4TD

1
The Magic Show

The show began. The curtains swished aside.

The stage appeared empty, then a spotlight beamed down revealing a blue pantomime horse. The horse had a moustache and wore a top hat. The

audience laughed. Music began and the horse did a little dance.

The music stopped. The horse looked up. A black box about the size of a freezer floated slowly down on almost invisible wires. It landed in the centre of the stage.

'Oooo!' said Joe, Laurie and Theo.

'Ahh!' said the rest of the audience.

The horse went up and sniffed the box. It lifted its leg like a dog, as if it were going to pee on it. Then it walked behind the box and disappeared.

Almost immediately the music started up again and this time, instead of the horse, Ivor Trick the magician appeared from behind the box!

The audience laughed and clapped.

Ivor Trick had dark eyes and a long black moustache. He swirled his cloak and stroked his chin. He stared right at

the three brothers in their seats.

'Ooh er . . . ' said Theo. He held tightly to his older brothers' hands.

Now a single spotlight lit up the black box. Ivor Trick pointed at it. 'This is a Disappearing Box,' he said. 'I need a volunteer to go in it! A brave volunteer who'll go into my Disappearing Box and . . . DISAPPEAR!'

Laurie stuck his hand in the air. Joe, who was the eldest of the three, pulled it down.

'Ah! There's a likely looking lad!' said Ivor Trick.

He seemed to point towards the three brothers, but actually he was pointing behind them, to a small boy with big ears. The small boy went up

onto the stage and everyone clapped.

'This is Wee Willie, my nephew,' said the magician. 'He is going into the box. Willie will disappear, he will become part of the cosmos, he will become nothing more than a mite of dust . . . Then I will magic him back to normality.'

Wee Willie grinned. 'Cool,' he said.

The magician opened the box and Wee Willie went in. The door was shut. He waved his magic wand.

'Into the cosmos!' he yelled. He threw open the door again. The box was empty. The audience gasped. Ivor Trick rattled his wand against the inside walls to prove they were solid. He twizzled the Disappearing Box round and round. There were no other doors, no way out, and yet the boy had vanished. Ivor Trick shut the door.

'That was real magic, wasn't it?' said Theo.

'Wish I'd been disappeared,' said Laurie.

'I wish you had too,' said Joe.

The audience was now calling for Wee Willie to reappear. They began a slow clap. 'We want Wee Willie! We want Wee Willie!'

'See, anyone can disappear someone,' said Joe. 'It's the getting them back that's hard.'

Ivor Trick muttered something magical, then he tapped the wand against the box and opened the door with a flourish. 'WEE WILLIE!' he cried.

The box was empty. Well, almost empty. On the floor were some of Wee Willie's clothes.

Ivor Trick slammed the door shut

again. He repeated his magic words. He opened the door. The Disappearing Box was still empty, only this time, as if from a long way off, they heard Wee Willie calling faintly, 'HELP! HELP!'

The audience began to worry and whisper.

'Where's that boy gone?' asked Theo.

'I don't know,' said Joe.

'Disappeared,' said Laurie.

Ivor Trick raced round the box yelling. He hit the box with his fist. He twirled his cloak. He threw his top hat on the floor.

'It's SABOTAGE!' he shouted. 'It was Daphne Davorski who did this to me! It's her box. She tricked me! Listen, I want you all to know, it was Daphne Davorski who did this to me! She's—'

The curtains swished together, but Ivor Trick tore his way through them to

the front of the stage. 'Daphne
Davorski lent me that box! She's tricked
me! She wants to ruin me!'

Daphne Davorski was the other
magician that the boys had come to
watch. Now she came onto the stage,
dressed, as she always was, as a witch.

'I'm innocent! I didn't do anything!'

she cried.

Ivor Trick knocked her pointed hat off with his wand. 'Liar!'

Daphne Davorski yanked Ivor Trick's moustache. 'Cheat!'

Then they both raised their wands and zapped each other with a magic spell.

'Halfwit!' yelled Ivor Trick.

'Horse brain!' yelled Daphne Davorski.

Their wands touched, sparked and fired. There was smoke and shrieks. The heavy fire curtain came down hiding them both from view. It was the end of the show.

2
The Croco-cat

The next day the three boys were walking back from the sweet shop. Joe was giving Theo a piggyback.

'I've just seen a witch,' said Theo. He peered over the privet hedge. 'She's sitting in a striped deckchair on her porch.'

'Silly,' said Joe. 'There's no such thing!'

'Daphne Davorski looks like a witch,'

said Laurie.

Joe stood very still. He let Theo slither down his back. 'You are right – for once. She does. Do you think that was her? Shall we go see?'

They went back along the road and peered over the hedge. Theo peered through the hedge.

The woman was still sitting on the porch. She was asleep. She had a very

big nose with a wart on it. Her chin was long, with a wart on it. Her bushy black eyebrows (with warts on) were as thick as the privet hedge. She had straggly black hair.

Beside her chair was a pointed black hat.

'A witch's hat! Told you!' squeaked Theo.

'Look in the window,' said Laurie. 'What is THAT?'

Standing between two potted geraniums, was a most extraordinary cat. Its face was black with white-tipped ears and long white whiskers. But halfway along, it became something green with very short legs. A crocodile.

'A croco-cat!' cried Theo. 'WOW! Great! I've always wanted a croco-cat!'

'Shut up, Theo!'

The witch woke up. 'Hey!' she yelled. 'You boys!'

"Let'sgetoutofhere!'

The boys ran.

* * *

The brothers had a tree house in their garden. They called it the Bed of Luck. Once their cousin Tommy fell out of it into the road but a passing stranger caught him. 'That was lucky!' said the passing stranger.

That's why they called it the Bed of Luck.

'Do you think that witch was Daphne Davorski?' said Joe.

'It looked like her,' said Laurie. 'She isn't a real witch, is she?'

'We could take Clinky Monkey along to sniff her,' said Theo. 'I bet he'd know if she was a real witch.'

Clinky Monkey was sitting below them on the grass, waiting for the boys to throw him some sweets. Clinky Monkey still wore the diamond collar that Timothy Potts-Smythe had made

for him. Joe and Laurie had tried and tried to make Theo sell it, but he refused.

The collar twinkled expensively in the sun. Theo threw the dog his lolly stick. Clinky Monkey chewed it up.

'Clinky Monkey wouldn't be able to smell a dead weasel at a hundred metres,' said Laurie.

'We need to get closer to her to see her clearly,' said Joe. 'We could go ask her if she wants any help with her garden or something. Like boy scouts do.'

'I don't think boy scouts still exist,' said Laurie.

'Are they instinct?' said Theo. 'Like dinosaurs?'

'Shut up, Theo,' said Joe and Laurie.

'All right,' said Theo. 'Can Clinky come too?'

'No,' said Joe. 'The witch will put a spell on him.'

'But you said she wasn't a witch.'

'Shut up, Theo.'

They went back to the house with the high privet hedge and the witch.

When they looked into the garden she wasn't there. The chair on the porch was empty. The witch's hat had gone. The croco-cat was not on the windowsill.

'Perhaps we made it all up?' said Laurie.

'I'm not clever enough to make up a witch sitting on a stripy deckchair,' said Theo.

'That's true,' said Laurie.

They heard a noise. Something or someone was making a rustling noise. Someone or something was creeping and sliding towards them in the flowerbed.

Theo yelped. 'It's the witch! She's

going to get me!'

'Don't be silly,' said Laurie.

'There is something!' said Joe. 'I see it . . . It's coming . . . '

Suddenly the witch popped up. She was inches away from them on the other side of the hedge.

Theo screamed.

'Don't scream!' shouted the witch. She grabbed Theo. Her long fingers wrapped around his little wrists. She tugged on him. 'Don't shout!'

The witch pulled Theo. Joe and Laurie held on to him, but the witch was terribly strong and she pulled Theo right through the hedge.

He disappeared in a flurry of privet leaves and twigs.

'THEO!'

The two bigger boys tried to push their way through the hedge after him,

but they were too large.

They dashed along the hedge looking for a gate or a way in. They couldn't see one. The hedge went on and on.

'Theo! Theo!'

At last they reached the gate. It was almost hidden in the thick leafy hedge. They struggled and struggled; finally they got it open. There was no sign of the witch or Theo.

They ran to the porch. It was empty. They tried the front door. It was locked.

'Round the back!' said Joe. He sprinted up the path, leaped over a bed of roses and ran towards the back garden. 'Mum'll never forgive us!' He jumped over a fallen wheelbarrow. 'Dad'll be so cross we've lost our little brother. Theo's scared of witches.'

'Theo's scared of everything!' Laurie added, racing along behind him.

'Oh, poor little Theo!'

'Poor little Theo!'

They ran. They were just in time to see the witch disappearing round the side of the house, taking Theo with her.

3
The Half-Witch

As Joe and Laurie raced across the lawn, the croco-cat streaked past. 'Miaow-snap!' it cried, flicking its green tail.

'Freaky!' said Joe.

There was a large conservatory on the back of the house. The witch was in there; so was Theo.

The boys burst in.

'Let go of Theo!' shouted Joe. 'You bully!'

'I'll call the police!' said Laurie.

The witch glared at them. She was so witchy it was scary to have to look at her at all.

Then a funny thing happened. The witch flopped down in a chair. Her pointed hat fell off. She burst into tears.

'I'm sorry, I'm sorry,' she said. 'I

didn't mean to frighten your little
brother.'

'You didn't,' said Theo. 'I just like
screaming.'

'I got carried away. I was thinking
about Wee Willie . . . '

'So you *are* Daphne Davorski!' said
Joe.

The witch nodded. 'Wee Willie is my
son. My darling little lambkin. I miss

him so. Please, please, let me explain,'
she said. 'Sit down. I'll get you a bit of
juice and some cakes.'

The witch blew her nose and went
out.

'Do you think it's safe?' said Laurie.

'No,' said Joe, grabbing Theo. 'Let's
run for it.'

''Course it's safe,' said Theo. 'Her
bottom bit's just like Mum.'

'What are you talking about, you silly
little boy?' said Joe.

'She's got jeans and red toenails and
sandals just like Mum,' said Theo. 'So
she must be kind, really.'

Joe made a face. 'You are so stupid,
Theo. Sometimes I wonder how you
got into this family.'

'I was invited,' said Theo. He folded
his arms. 'Mum invited me.'

'Shut up, Theo,' said Laurie.

'You look like you've been dragged backwards through a hedge,' said Joe.

'Frontwards,' said Laurie.

The witch came back. 'Here.' She put a plate of odd-looking éclairs down on the table. 'It's all I can offer you. Half a glass of juice and half an éclair.'

Joe picked up his glass. The glass was half a blue mug. It was half-full of juice. He picked up an éclair. It was half an éclair and half something else.

'It's just half a slug,' said the witch. 'The other bit's OK.'

Joe put the éclair back on the plate. It slowly slithered off the plate and oozed onto the table. 'I like slugs,' said Joe. 'But not enough to eat one. Thank you.'

'Try the buns.' She handed Theo a bun. The bun jumped out of his hand and leaped out of the door. Half of the bun was an iced cake with half a cherry on top. The other half was a frog. 'Ribbet-sponge! Ribbet-sponge!' it croaked from the flowerbed.

'It's a half-spell,' said the witch, 'and half of it's all wrong anyway.'

'Did Ivor Trick do this to you last night?' said Laurie. 'We watched the show.'

'Did you?' The witch brightened up. 'You saw it? You saw what my brother did? He disappeared my little boy – his own nephew! Then he blamed me! Then he zapped me with a spell which was rubbish – half this, half that! And I zapped him–'

'What magic trick did you do on him?' asked Theo.

'I horsed him,' said Daphne, with a

smile. 'Only it was rubbish too because the magic got its wires crossed right in the middle so I don't think it worked at all . . . '

'Oh dear,' said Laurie. 'What a mess.'

'Yes. And me! I am only half a witch, as your brother noticed; my bottom bit is normal. The kitchen isn't half a mess!'

'Isn't half a mess or is half a mess?' asked Laurie.

'Can we see it?' said Joe.

The witch led them into the kitchen. The kettle was half a cauldron. The jar of pickled onions was pickled eyeballs.

There were snakes in the cutlery drawer.

'It's bad, isn't it? Such a mess,' said the witch. 'And then there's me.' She looked down at herself. 'I look awful!' She burst into tears again.

4
The Magic Circle

The witch, who was only half a witch, sat down at the kitchen table, which was only half a kitchen table. The other half was a large tank of water with fish in it. 'Watch your fingers, boys,' she warned them. 'Piranhas!'

'Wow!' said Laurie. 'Can I have one for a pet?'

'No,' said Joe.

'Be careful, the table wobbles,' said the witch. 'Mind you don't get wet. I must fix it . . . Oh, I'm at my wits' end,' she went on.

'Or half-witted?' suggest Joe.

Luckily the half-witch laughed.

'Ivor did that trick to make me look bad – he knows I'm a better magician than he is and he's trying to get me thrown out of the Magic Circle,' she said. 'He's jealous.'

'What's the Magic Circle?'

'You do ask a lot of questions, Theo.'

'Do I ask a lot of questions?' said Theo.

'There you go again,' said the half-witch. 'The Magic Circle is the society of the top magicians in the country – a sort of club. A magician has to be a member of the Magic Circle to work. I don't care about that though, I just want Wee Willie back.'

'And he's still inside your Disappearing Box,' said Joe.

'Yes. And Ivor has taken the box... He's probably got the box hidden at his shop – it's just in the village you know . . . There's no point in me going . . . but if you were to get a chance to snoop around in there . . . '

'We're good at snooping,' said Joe. 'You can count on us.'

'Thank you.'

While Joe and Laurie cleared the table, Theo went into the garden. He watched the slug-éclair crawling along the path. That'll make a nice surprise for a blackbird, he thought. He found half a good, straight, shiny black stick. It looked like a bit of a magic wand. The other half of the black stick was a

banana, so he ate that.

Joe and Laurie came out.

'I've found half a magic wand,' said Theo.

'You are so silly,' said Joe. 'People don't leave magic wands just lying around the place.'

'They do,' said Theo, 'because I've just found one.'

'Shut up, Theo,' said Joe and Laurie.

They stopped beside the gate to

watch the jumping bun.

'What a stupid thing a jumping bun is,' said Joe.

'Yeah, half-baked,' said Laurie.

'I wonder where Wee Willie went,' said Joe. 'D'you think he really is a dot of dust now – part of the cosmos?'

'Nah! I think Ivor Trick cut him in half, or maybe quarters!'

'If he had, Wee Willie would be even more wee than when he started,' said Joe. 'He'd be wee wee.'

5
Ivor Trick's Magic Shop

Theo got dressed up as a magician. He tied his mum's apron round his neck as a cloak. His new half-wand was sleek and very black, but it was too short. It didn't feel quite right when he magicked things with it. Theo found a long knobbly stick instead. It didn't look anything like a magic wand, but at least it was longer. He swirled it over C l i n k y M o n k e y to make h i m vanish.

Clinky Monkey did not want to vanish and ate the stick instead.

'Now you'll never join the Magic Circle,' said Joe.

'I never wanted to. I'm going to join the Magic Square,' said Theo.

'Ha, ha.'

They all watched Clinky Monkey shredding the stick.

'Time to go into the village and find a new magic wand,' said Laurie.

'Totally brilliant idea,' said Joe.

In the village they saw a notice pinned to a tree:

IVOR TRICK'S WONDERFUL
WIZARD & WITCH
☆☆ STORE ☆
Buy all your magic trickery
here →

The arrow pointed down a narrow cobbled alleyway.

They went down the alley. At the end they came to a small, dark shop that looked crumpled and squeezed, as if the houses on either side didn't like it and were saying mean things to it. The shop window was very dusty; they could just make out some pointed hats, capes with stars and moons on and a plastic cauldron sitting on some pretend hot orange coals.

'Freaky,' said Joe. 'Let's go in.'

A bell tinkled as they pushed the door open. It was dark inside.

On the counter there were jars of shrunken rats and spongy eyeballs. There was a tray of rubber fingers with nails stuck through them. The shelves were stacked with grubby boxes: smoking moustaches, soap to blacken

your face, stick-on warts, crystal balls (big and extra big), snake skins, poison darts, ingredients for potions and other interesting things.

A string of false noses dangled above the counter.

A row of pretend heads lined the very top shelf. Each one had a funny hat with false hair attached to it. Some had warts and twisted mouths and bolts through their necks. Clinky Monkey hid behind Theo and growled at them.

Theo pointed at a small boy stuck flat against the wall. 'Look at him!'

It wasn't actually a boy, but a set of boy's clothes pinned on the wall. Jumper and shirt, trousers with pants just showing, socks, shoes: the lot. Where his face should have been, there was a photograph of Wee Willie.

Above the flat boy was this notice:

There was a sort of long, slow whinnying sound. The boys spun round.

It was Ivor Trick.

6
Ivor Trick

'Neeehar! Neeehar!'

Ivor Trick looked much taller behind the counter than he had on stage. His face seemed longer. His lips were rubbery and moved about a lot over his long yellow teeth.

'Neeehar? Well?' He popped a sugar lump into his mouth and crunched it loudly. 'Yes?' He leaned over the counter like a horse leaning over a stable door. His nostrils quivered as if they smelled something – a crunchy apple maybe?

'Have you seen that boy?' He nodded at the clothes on the wall. 'My nephew. My dear little Willie?'

'No!'

'Are you sure? Are you positive?' His wobbly lips wrinkled. 'Your denial sounds a little half-hearted to me. You sound as if you may be telling me a half-truth.'

'No, no, we're not,' said Joe.

'We've come to buy a wand,' said Theo. 'Have you got any? Clinky Monkey ate mine.'

'A monkey ate your wand? You think

I'm half-awake perhaps? You have no monkey!'

'That's right,' said Theo, smiling.

The magician looked from one boy to the next and back again. 'I don't very much like your manner,' he said.

'I haven't got a manner and I want a wand,' said Theo.

'Yes, I understood that part,' said Ivor Trick. 'And I shall get you one. The cheapest, I presume?'

'Yes,' said Theo. 'One that Clinky Monkey won't eat.'

Ivor Trick made a face. 'No animal would eat one of my wands, I am sure.' The magician laughed. It sounded like a horse neighing. The three boys grinned, then tried to hide their grins.

'Neigh-ho!' said Joe.

'Clip, clop. Clip, clop,' said Theo, patting the counter absent-mindedly.

'Time gallops on,' said Laurie, tapping his feet.

Ivor Trick stared at them as if they were mad. He eyed Clinky Monkey suspiciously. 'Is that dog wearing a diamond collar?' he said.

'Yes,' said Theo.

'No,' said Joe.

'No,' said Laurie. 'Of course not.'

Ivor Trick sneered at Theo. 'I knew they weren't real,' he said. 'No dog walks around Bristow wearing a diamond collar.'

'Clinky Monkey does,' said Theo. 'So there.'

'Shut up, Theo!' said Joe and Laurie.

Ivor Trick lifted the counter up and stepped into the main part of the shop. 'Your dog isn't dangerous, is he?' he asked.

'Yes,' said all three boys, hopefully.

Clinky Monkey wagged his tail and grinned in a friendly way.

Ivor Trick opened a cupboard. Inside were boxes and boxes of wands. They were labelled:

Cheap and nasty plastic.
Cheap Plastic.
nasty plastic.
Expensive.
Ones that Really Work.

'Can we have one that really works?' asked Joe.

'Of course you can't!' snapped Ivor Trick. 'They are only for members of the Magic Circle.'

'Psst!' Laurie nudged Joe. He pointed into the cupboard at a black square thing.

The black square thing looked like a folded bit of cardboard, about the size of a CD case. On it was written: **Magic Disappearing Box** and in small letters: This box belongs to Daphne Davorski. And in even smaller letters, Folding Flip Flap Flat Pack.

'Cool!' Joe mouthed silently.

Ivor pushed the Disappearing Box further back in the cupboard. 'Noses out!'

He took out a cheap and nasty plastic wand and handed it to Theo. 'Your

47

Clinky Monkey would have to like eating toxic plastic and sharp metal, to get through that!'

Theo nodded sadly. 'He does,' he said. 'I'd better have two, please.'

'Ridiculous child!'

Ivor Trick gave Theo two wands and shut the cupboard up. He went back round to the other side of the counter. He quivered his nostrils at them.

'Money, please!' Ivor Trick held out his hand, palm flat. It had a sugar lump on it. 'Whoops!' He ate the sugar lump quickly. 'Though how I can think about money under these tragic circumstances, I'll never know,' he added.

'How can you then?' asked Laurie. 'Hey?'

'Hay is what horses eat!' said Ivor.

Laurie and Joe sniggered.

'Life must go on,' went on Ivor,

wiping a tear from his eye. 'Even without my Wee Willie by my side.'

Theo giggled.

Joe and Laurie exchanged a secret, meaningful look.

'I feel ill,' said Laurie. Suddenly he crumpled to the floor. 'I need water, water . . . water . . . '

'Oh, dear, my brother's ill,' said Joe. 'He needs water, water . . . '

Ivor Trick snorted. 'For goodness sake!' he cried. 'Why must the boy collapse here, in my shop? Why?'

'Maybe he likes it here,' said Theo.

'No, it's because he's a pain in the neck!' said Ivor. 'I'll go and get some water from the kitchen. DO NOT TOUCH ANYTHING!'

As soon as Ivor Trick was gone, Joe opened the cupboard, snatched the Disappearing Box and stuffed it down

his jeans.

Ivor Trick was back five seconds later. Laurie jumped up and took the glass of water. He gulped it down quickly. 'Thank you so much,' he said, grinning. 'Do you have any oats or bran I could munch on?'

'Oats? Bran? Are you mad?' yelled Ivor Trick. 'Give me the money for the wands and get out!'

The boys paid up and got out.

7
The Magic Disappearing Box

As soon as they were back home Joe, Laurie and Theo went up into the Bed of Luck. Theo threw down one of the magic wands to Clinky Monkey. Clinky Monkey ate it in twenty-six seconds. They timed him.

'I told Ivor Trick that Clinky would do that,' said Theo. He shook his head.

'That Ivor Trick is a fraud and a cheat and half a horse too,' said Joe.

Laurie giggled and made clip-clop noises. 'Show us the box, Joe.'

Joe took out the Disappearing Box. He turned it over a few times. 'Wee Willie can't be in there . . . can he? Wonder how it works?'

'It says "Pull Here",' said Laurie. He pulled 'Pull Here'.

The box quietly exploded.

It flipped and flapped and flopped and unfolded. The sides whooshed up. The edges zipped and zapped. The ends popped out and up and over. It grew so big and so quickly that the boys had to scramble out of the way.

'Watch out!' yelled Joe.

The Disappearing Box toppled out of the Bed of Luck. It fell out of the tree. It somersaulted and landed right on top of Clinky Monkey.

'*Weroof!*'

'Oh no!'

The boys scrambled down as quickly as they could, but their dog had gone! Vanished.

There wasn't even a distant, muffled bark coming from it.

'Clinky Monkey! Clinky Monkey!' Theo yelled. 'Come back!' He hit the box with his cheap and nasty plastic wand. 'Come back!'

'We'll have to go in!' said Laurie.

'But we may never come out again,' said Joe. 'We'll be stuck, just like Wee Willie.'

'But we'll be with Clinky Monkey,' said Theo.

They opened the small door. Their way was barred by black velvet. They pushed it aside and walked in.

The disappearing box was like Dr

Who's Tardis: it was much bigger on the
inside than the outside.

'Spooky,' said Joe. He held Theo's
hand.

'Cool!' said Laurie. He held Theo's
other hand. 'It's like a church hall.'

It *was* just like a church hall. It even
smelled of old mashed potato and
sweaty gym shoes like some church

halls do. The floor was very dusty. The walls were festooned with fading posters advertising long-gone bazaars and magic shows. There was a grand piano with broken keys. Bits of discarded clothing lay around. A yellowing newspaper fluttered as they went by.

They walked on and on, opening door after door and passing through hall after hall, after boring, dusty, hall.

'Clinky Monkey! Clinky Monkey!' they called.

They passed two miserable-looking rabbits hopping in the opposite direction. Four white doves flew gently over their heads like little kites. The place felt sad and empty.

Theo picked up half a black stick with a band of silver round it.

'Look! Hey, look! It's the other bit of

my magic wand!' He fitted it to his half-wand he'd found in Daphne Davorski's garden. 'I bet it'll work now. I bet when I mend it properly, it will be as good as a real magic wand.'

'Don't be stupid, Theo,' said Joe.

They walked on.

An abandoned top hat and black silk gloves lay in one corner, covered in cobwebs. Laurie found a pack of cards in another. He picked them up; they were all glued together and fell in a long stream, like a scarf.

'What a gloomy sort of place this is,' said Joe. 'A place for mistakes. For half-done tricks and performances. I feel really sorry for little Wee Willie being stuck in here.'

Suddenly they heard a bark.

'It's Clinky!' And the boys rushed off towards him.

8
Wee Willie

Clinky Monkey was at the very end of the last vast hall. He was wearing a little pointed hat with a star on it. He wagged his tail and barked.

Beside him, crouching in the shadows, was a small naked boy: Wee Willie. He was shivering and his grubby face was streaked from crying.

'At last!' he cried. 'I'm saved!' He stood up wrapping a red silk hanky round his middle.

'Wee Willie?' asked Joe.

'You can't see that from here,' said Laurie.

The brothers giggled.

The naked boy didn't laugh. 'Yes, I'm Wee Willie. I've been waiting for ages and ages for someone to come and find me. Why didn't Uncle Ivor come and get me? I'm cold and I'm hungry and I'm totally, totally fed up and miserable and . . . Is this black and white dog yours?'

'Yes,' said Theo. He slipped his hand through Clinky Monkey's collar. 'You can't have him, he's mine.'

'Oh, I hoped he was a stray.' Wee Willie looked sad. 'I think he'd make a wonderful dog in a magic routine, with that hat and the diamonds and everything.'

'They're not real diamonds,' said Joe. 'Of course.'

'Of course,' said Wee Willie. 'But if you ever want to hire him out . . . '

'No,' said Theo.

'My mum is Daphne Davorski, she's quite a good magician and my uncle is Ivor Trick,' said Wee Willie. 'He's rich. He'd pay you lots and lots. He's very good at magic.'

'If your uncle, the great magician Ivor Trick, is so brilliant,' said Joe, 'how come he hasn't got you out of here?'

'I don't know,' said Wee Willie.

'OK, then we'll rescue you, seeing as no one else is doing it,' said Laurie.

'How?' asked Wee Willie. He stared round at the bleak room.

'We'll just go back the way we came in,' said Joe. 'Easy.'

They turned round and walked back towards the entrance. They went through hall after dusty hall. They went past the top hat and gloves and the rabbits and the grand piano. They came to the last hall, but the entrance – or exit

– had vanished.

They stopped, turned round and went back. They padded softly over the bare boards. The air was dusty and dead.

'I don't like it in here,' said Theo. 'I want to go home.'

'Soon, soon,' said Joe. 'Hmmm,' he added, after a long while of wandering around, 'we appear to be stuck.'

'We have disappeared,' said Laurie.

'We're part of the cosmos,' said Wee Willie.

'Gone,' said Joe. 'Vanished.'

'I can still see you,' said Theo. 'And I can see me.'

'But we have disappeared to the rest of the world,' said Joe.

Wee Willie started sobbing. 'I hate this place! I want to get out of here. I hate it! We're all going to die! We're doomed!'

'Hush, hush,' said Laurie. 'My brother is going to have a good idea, any minute . . . now!'

'I've got an idea,' said Joe. 'This box is only made of folding paper, so we should be able to cut our way out.' He pushed against the wall. 'Ouch! That hurt. It's like stone!'

'I'm nearly, very, very, a little bit scared,' said Theo. His bottom lip was trembling.

'Hey! Now I *do* have an idea,' said Joe. 'Remember that sort of rhyme we used to say? The one about the horse and the saw? You know! You *must* remember!'

The others shook their heads.

'We rub our hands until they're *sore*,' said Joe. 'Use the *saw* to cut a hole in the wall. Shout until we're *hoarse*. Climb on

61

the *horse* and gallop away!'

The other boys stared at him, open-mouthed. Laurie yelled, 'Yes! Brilliant!' He began feverishly rubbing his hands together.

Joe and Theo and Wee Willie did the same.

No saw appeared.

'OK, I'll try shouting,' said Joe.

He shouted and shouted until he was hoarse. He stopped as he heard the sound of pattering feet approaching.

'It worked. Here comes a horse!'

But it wasn't a horse, it was the two sad rabbits lolloping along.

'Oh, well, it was a good idea,' said Joe. 'Better than anything any of you could think of.'

'Maybe . . . ' Laurie picked up a piece of paper from the floor. It had been torn roughly and had a jagged edge.

'What's this?'

'It's a piece of paper, you dimwit,' said Joe.

Theo picked up another scrap of paper. It was also torn down the side.

'Mmm, this puzzle is all about halves,' said Laurie. 'Half a witch, half a bun, half a— '

'Brain,' said Joe.

'Half a wand,' said Theo. 'I've got—'

'Shut up, Theo!'

'Two halves make a whole,' said Laurie. He held the torn piece of paper up against Theo's bit of paper and they fitted together perfectly.

'A whole!'

'And we could escape through a hole,' said Joe. He pressed the two pieces together neatly against the wall. 'Now what?'

'You need magic,' said Wee Willie.

'I'll use my magic wand,' said Theo. 'It's two halves as well.'

'Shut up, Theo. That's a dumb idea!'

Theo ignored him. He held the two bits of the magic wand together in his fist.

'Say the magic word!' said Wee Willie.

'Please!' said Theo.

'No, the other one,' said Joe.

'Abracadabra!'

Theo tapped the paper with his wand.

Immediately the paper burst into flames leaving a gaping hole in the wall. Sunshine streamed through. They could see their garden and their tree house.

'Yahoo!' 'We're free!'

9
Tricking Ivor Trick

The boys tore at the wall and made the hole bigger and climbed out into the fresh air.

The four doves flew out after them and settled in the Bed of Luck. They cooed contentedly.

'Told you it was a magic wand,' said Theo.

Nobody told him to shut up.

'Fresh air!' cried Wee Willie. 'Sunshine!' He skipped and leaped around like a lamb. Then he saw the tree house. 'Can I go up? Can I? I've never been in a tree house!'

He climbed up into the Bed of Luck and sat there swinging his legs and singing about tulips and bluebirds.

Suddenly a voice called loudly,

'Thieves! THIEVES!'

It was Ivor Trick.

'You've stolen the Disappearing Box? Thieves! Scoundrels!'

THIEVES!
THIEVES!

Joe, Laurie and Theo stood beside the Disappearing Box and tried not to look up at Wee Willie, who was attempting to hide in the leaves.

'Your box is just here,' said Joe,

pointing at the box.

'So I can see! You *stole* that box. I shall report you to the police!'

'Oh, yes, good idea,' said Joe. 'But, before you do, we must tell you, we heard someone inside the box. Calling.'

'Did you?' Ivor Trick looked worried.

'Yes. A boy's voice, wasn't it, Joe?' said Laurie.

'Yes,' said Joe. 'The boy's voice said he'd found some gold . . . a gold box or . . . a gold coin . . . ' He pretended to look puzzled.

'I thought he said a *big* box of gold coins,' said Laurie.

'But it was hard to tell . . . ' added Joe.

'He sounded ever so excited,' said Theo.

'Well, *we* were excited,' said Joe.

'We were just going to go in—' said Laurie.

'Whoa, whoa! Steady on,' said Ivor
Trick. He held his arm out to stop the
boys going any closer to the box. 'Don't
be hasty, boys. Rein yourselves in.
Whoa! *I'll* go in.'

"Fraid you can't,' said Joe. 'You're too
big.'

'I think not,' said Ivor Trick.

'I'm sure you'll never fit,' said Laurie.
'*We* should go in.'

'I feel it is my duty to try,' said Ivor
Trick. 'I am the only adult here. Gold

you said? Lots of it? Can't let you boys endanger your lives. Think of your parents. Now, if I could just . . . '

Ivor Trick got down on his knees. He squashed his shoulder in. He tucked his chin down onto his chest. He squeezed himself through the small doorway and disappeared.

'I shan't let you down!' he called over his shoulder.

'But we'll let YOU down!' yelled Joe. 'Go on, Theo!'

Theo hit the Disappearing Box with his magic wand. 'Abracadabra!'

Immediately the box began to collapse. It flipped, flapped and flopped. The edges slipped and slid. The sides wheezed and sighed. The walls folded and bent and pleated. The roof caved in and tucked down and under and away. The ends flipped over and the top flapped down.

In ten seconds all that remained of the Magic Disappearing Box was a flat black square, like a CD case, lying on the grass.

'Hey, Theo,' said Joe. 'That was something.'

'It was,' said Theo.

'A fitting punishment,' said Joe.

'A flatting punishment,' said Laurie.

'Those poor rabbits,' said Joe, shaking his head. 'We should have saved them.'

'They'll be all right,' said Laurie. 'Bunnies are used to getting squashed.'

'It's OK,' said Theo. He rolled up his jumper. 'I've got them safe.' He put the rabbits down on the grass. The rabbits perked up. Their noses twitched. They hopped over the lawn and started nibbling the grass. 'Mum'll like them,' said Theo. 'She's always wanted rabbits.'

Joe picked up the folding flip flap flat box and tucked it in his pocket.

'You can come down now, Wee Willie!' Laurie called.

'That was great!' said Wee Willie. 'Serves Uncle Ivor right to be stuck in there. Let's see how he likes being a dot in the cosmos.'

'Let's go and tell Daphne Davorski the good news,' said Joe.

'First I need some clothes,' said Wee Willie, clutching his red hanky. 'Please.'

10
Daphne Davorski

Theo mended his magic wand with sticky tape. When he flipped it around he was sure he saw tiny stars flying from its tip. He didn't tell his brothers.

'Don't eat this wand,' he warned Clinky Monkey. 'This one works!'

Theo put the magic wand down his trouser leg and held it in place with his hand in his pocket. He knew if he didn't hide such a splendid wand, someone would take it.

* * *

'Mum! Mum! It's me!' Wee Willie leaped into Daphne

Davorski's arms.

'Willie!' Daphne Davorski hugged him and smothered him with kisses. 'You're safe! My dear little boy.'

Joe whispered to Laurie, 'I'm surprised Wee Willie can even recognise her with that awful face and the warts, but to actually kiss her! Yick!'

'Yuck,' said Laurie.

'I am so happy! Thank you, boys,' said Daphne Davorski. 'Splendid work!' She slapped the table. The table wobbled and water splashed over. The piranha snapped their teeth.

'Whoops! I should get that mended,' said the half-witch. 'But without my wand, I'm a broken woman.'

'Half a woman,' said Joe.

'A woman in two halves?' said Laurie.

'I suspect Ivor Trick stole it,' said Daphne Davorski. 'It's a black and pointy wand with a silver band. Ivor halved it . . . I don't suppose you've seen it, have you?'

Joe, Laurie and Wee Willie all stared at Theo.

Theo shook his head. He bit his lip. He blinked very fast. He stared at the ceiling. He stared at his feet where a half-bun, half-frog was sitting. Theo squeezed the magic wand, which was still down his trouser leg and said, 'Abracadabra!'

The frog-bun exploded in a shower of tiny stars, like a quiet firework. When the smoke cleared, there was an iced bun on the toe of Theo's trainer.

'You've found it!' cried Daphne Davorski. 'You've got my wand! Goody! Now I shall put things right!'

Theo handed her the wand. 'Can I join the Magic Circle?'

'You're too young. You could join the Magic Semi-Circle, that's for little people.'

'No, thank you,' said Theo. 'I don't think I like rice pudding.'

'You're thinking of semolina, it's not the same,' said Joe.

Theo made a face. 'I don't believe you.'

The half-witch waved her magic wand. Everything snapped and flared and lit up brightly as they changed back to what they'd been. There was the smell of burning and soft sizzling noises in the air. It was like Guy Fawkes night, only quieter.

'Oh,' said Theo. 'I wanted to do that.'

Daphne Davorski had changed herself too. She was not a half-witch any longer. Her jeans and red toenails and blue jeans had disappeared. Now she was dressed in a long black skirt and pointed black boots.

She was a whole witch.

'Don't be frightened,' said Daphne Davorski. 'People think I put this disguise on when I go on stage but it's the real me. I can't help it. Have a bun?'

The buns did not jump anymore. The éclairs did not slither. There were no piranhas in the kitchen table.

'Well, that's the end of that,' said the whole witch. 'Except for Ivor Trick! What shall we do about him?'

'Oh, I forgot,' said Joe. 'Ivor's trapped in your Disappearing Box. Here it is.'

'Yahoo!' cried Daphne Davorski. 'Brilliant! Well done, boys . . . But,' she paused, 'what shall I do with it?'

There was silence.

Daphne looked at Wee Willie.

Joe looked at Laurie.

Theo looked at Clinky Monkey.

Clinky Monkey looked at Daphne

Davorski's juicy magic wand.

'I know,' said Joe. He took the box and pushed it under the wobbly table leg. 'There you are,' he said. 'Even Ivor can be of use, can't he?'

Daphne Davorski gave the boys more cakes and drink, then everyone said goodbye and thank you and the brothers set off for home.

As they went out of the gate Theo heard the croco-cat.

'Miaow-snap, miaow-snap.'

Theo picked the cat up. It didn't have a swishy green tail anymore but it still looked rather odd. It had a long, pointed nose covered in black fur. It had long white whiskers. It had a crocodile grin and sneaky crocodile eyes. The cat cuddled into Theo's arms and purred and purred.

'Mum will love him,' said Theo.

'What makes you think that?' asked Laurie.

'Because I love him and Clinky Monkey loves him.'

'You could magic yourself as many cats and crocodiles as you wanted if you had a real magic wand,' said Joe.

'But I haven't got one,' said Theo.

'If you sold Clinky Monkey's diamond collar,' said Joe, 'you could buy twenty real wands that really work.'

'No,' said Theo.

'But—'

'Clinky Monkey's the only dog in the whole of Bristow with a diamond collar,' said Theo. 'That's how I want it.'

And so that's how it was.